The
BEAR UNDER THE STAIRS

story and pictures by Helen Cooper

A Puffin Pied Piper

For Ted

PUFFIN BOOKS
Published by the Penguin Group
Penguin Books USA Inc., 375 Hudson Street, New York, New York 10014, U.S.A.
Penguin Books Ltd, 27 Wrights Lane, London W8 5TZ, England
Penguin Books Australia Ltd, Ringwood, Victoria, Australia
Penguin Books Canada Ltd, 10 Alcorn Avenue, Toronto, Ontario, Canada M4V 3B2
Penguin Books (N.Z.) Ltd, 182-190 Wairau Road, Auckland 10, New Zealand

Penguin Books Ltd, Registered Offices: Harmondsworth, Middlesex, England

First published in Great Britain by Doubleday
A Division of Transworld Publishers Ltd
First published in the United States of America by Dial Books for Young Readers,
a division of Penguin Books USA Inc., 1993
Published in Puffin Books, 1997

1 3 5 7 9 10 8 6 4 2

THE LIBRARY OF CONGRESS HAS CATALOGED THE DIAL EDITION AS FOLLOWS:
Cooper, Helen F.
The bear under the stairs / written and illustrated by Helen Cooper.   p.   cm.
Summary: A little boy throws food below the stairs of his house each day
to appease the bear he believes lives there.
ISBN 0-8037-1279-0
[1. Fear—Fiction. 2. Imagination—Fiction. 3. Bears—Fiction.] I. Title.
PZ7.C7855Be 1993 [E]—dc20 92-23840 CIP AC

Puffin Books ISBN 0-14-056094-7

Printed in the United States of America

William was scared of grizzly bears,
and William was scared of the
place under the stairs.

It was all because
one day he thought
he saw a bear,
hiding there,
under the stairs.

And so he slammed the
door quick —
wham, bang, thump!

After that, William worried about the bear.
He wondered what it might eat.
"Yum, yum," he thought he heard the
bear whisper. "I'm a very hungry bear,
and maybe I'll eat a boy for lunch."

So William saved a pear for the bear
that lived there, under the stairs.

And when no one was watching,
William crept down the hall,
cracked open the door,
threw the pear to the bear
that lived under the stairs,
and slammed the door quick —
wham, bang, thump!

William had kept his eyes shut tight,
so he didn't actually see the bear
in its lair
under the stairs. . . .

But he knew what it looked like!

And at night

while William dreamed . . .

Every day William fed
the bear that lived
under the stairs.

He fed it bananas, bacon, and bread.

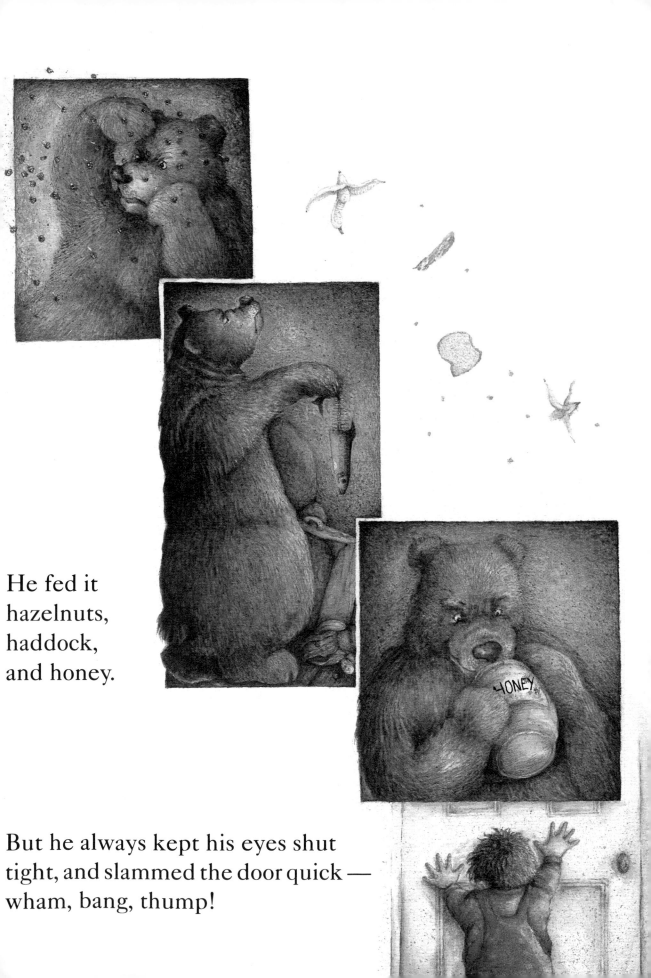

He fed it
hazelnuts,
haddock,
and honey.

But he always kept his eyes shut
tight, and slammed the door quick —
wham, bang, thump!

After a while there was a strange smell
in the air
near the bear
under the stairs.
The smell got stronger and stronger . . .

until William's mom noticed it.
"What's that awful smell!" she said.
"It seems to be coming
from there, under the stairs.
I think I'd better take a look."

"NO!"

shouted William, very scared.

"Don't go in there!"

"William, what's the matter?" Mom asked
as she lifted him onto her lap.
So William told her all about the hungry bear
in its lair, there, under the stairs.

Then William and Mom decided to scare
the bear that lived under the stairs.
William bravely kept his eyes wide open
this time,
and when they opened the door
he saw . . .

an old furry rug,
a broken chair,
and horrible stinky food everywhere . . .
but no scary bear!

So William and Mom
cleaned up the mess
under the stairs.

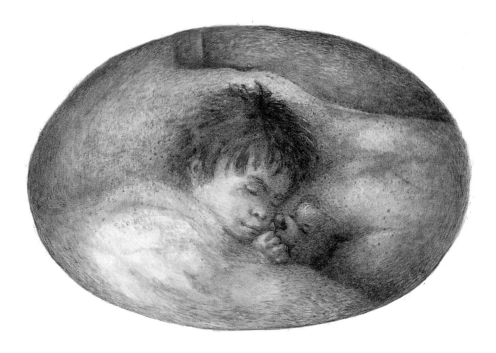

Then they went shopping and Mom
bought William a little brown grizzly
bear of his own. It had such a nice
face that William was never scared of bears . . .

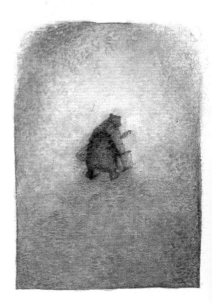

or the place under the stairs, ever again.